Dear Parents:

Congratulations! Your child is taking the first steps on an exciting journey. The destination? Independent reading!

STEP INTO READING® will help your child get there. The program offers five steps to reading success. Each step includes fun stories and colorful art or photographs. In addition to original fiction and books with favorite characters, there are Step into Reading Non-Fiction Readers, Phonics Readers and Boxed Sets, Sticker Readers, and Comic Readers—a complete literacy program with something to interest every child.

Learning to Read, Step by Step!

Ready to Read   Preschool–Kindergarten
• big type and easy words • rhyme and rhythm • picture clues
For children who know the alphabet and are eager to begin reading.

Reading with Help   Preschool–Grade 1
• basic vocabulary • short sentences • simple stories
For children who recognize familiar words and sound out new words with help.

Reading on Your Own   Grades 1–3
• engaging characters • easy-to-follow plots • popular topics
For children who are ready to read on their own.

Reading Paragraphs   Grades 2–3
• challenging vocabulary • short paragraphs • exciting stories
For newly independent readers who read simple sentences with confidence.

Ready for Chapters   Grades 2–4
• chapters • longer paragraphs • full-color art
For children who want to take the plunge into chapter books but still like colorful pictures.

STEP INTO READING® is designed to give every child a successful reading experience. The grade levels are only guides; children will progress through the steps at their own speed, developing confidence in their reading.

Remember, a lifetime love of reading starts with a single step!

Step into Reading, Random House, and the Random House colophon are registered trademarks of Penguin Random House LLC.

Visit us on the Web!
StepIntoReading.com
rhcbooks.com

Educators and librarians, for a variety of teaching tools, visit us at RHTeachersLibrarians.com

ISBN 978-0-7364-4363-0 (trade) — ISBN 978-0-7364-9033-7 (lib. bdg.)
ISBN 978-0-7364-4364-7 (ebook)

Printed in the United States of America

10 9 8 7 6 5 4 3 2 1

DISNEY · PIXAR

Bug Trouble!

by Steve Behling

illustrated by the Disney Storybook Art Team

Random House 🏠 New York

Captain Buzz Lightyear,
Izzy, Mo, Darby, and Sox
are ready for action.

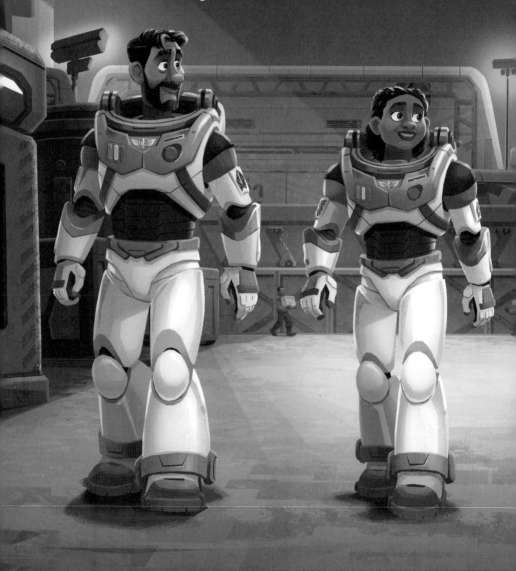

It is their first
Space Rangers mission.

The team meets
Commander Burnside.
He tells them their mission.

He shows the team
their new ship.
They need to go to the
dark side of the planet.

The team is excited!

They board the new ship.

Buzz tells his team to
remember their training.

Blastoff!

The ride is very smooth.

The ship lands.

Mo is excited.

He runs from the ship.
Sox and Darby chase
after him.

The team finds Mo.
Mo finds a glowing
purple orb on the ground.

They hear a
buzzing sound.
They are surrounded
by bugs!

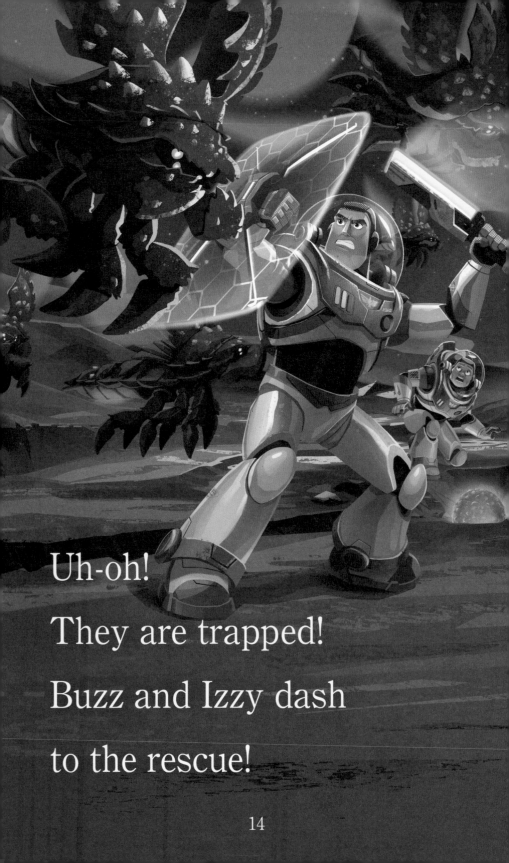

Uh-oh!
They are trapped!
Buzz and Izzy dash
to the rescue!

They have shields
and laser blades.
The bugs fly away.

Izzy tells Mo and Darby
not to run.
A team must
stick together!

Sox scans the orb.
He does not know
what it is.
The buzzing comes back.
There are more bugs!

But the bugs do not
attack the team.

The bugs want the orb.

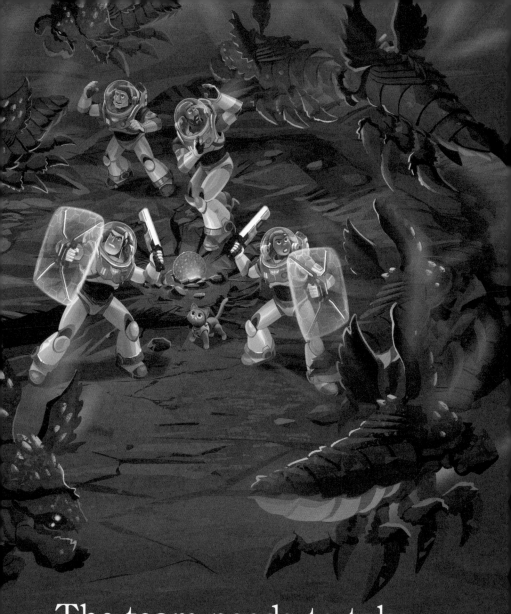

The team needs to take
the orb to Star Command.
Can they do it?

Izzy has an idea!
She tells the team
to use their flares.
They fire into
the sky!

The flares create
a bright light.
The bugs fly toward it.
Izzy's plan worked!

Suddenly, everything
goes dark.
What is happening?
Buzz is not worried.

The lights turn back on.

It was only a test.

The team never left

Star Command!

Buzz is proud of his team.
They did a great job!
They can solve any
problem by working
together!